STEP INTO **W9-CVA-249**

2
STEP
READING WITH HELP

nickelodeon

BUBBLE POWER!

BUBBLE GUPPIES

by Josephine Nagaraj
illustrated by MJ Illustrations
cover illustration colored by Steve Talkowski

Random House 🏠 New York

Guppy Girl
and Bubble Boy
are Super Guppies!
They wear masks
and capes.

Sid is a bad guy.

He collects

stinky smells.

6

Stinky garbage.

Rotten eggs.

Smelly socks.

Sid invents

a stink ray!

Sid wants
to fill
Big Bubble City
with stinky smells!

He fills a cloud
with stink sauce.

The police try
to stop Sid.
Sid sprays
stink sauce
on them!

This is a job
for Guppy Girl
and Bubble Boy!

Guppy Girl has

water power.

Bubble Boy has
bubble power.

The two heroes
spray water and
bubbles at Sid!

Sid is too strong!
He sprays them
with his stink ray.

Bubble Boy tries
to shut off
the stink machine.
He gets stinked!

Sid fires
his stink ray
at Guppy Girl.

But it is not her.
It is a paper cutout.
Guppy Girl has
tricked Sid!

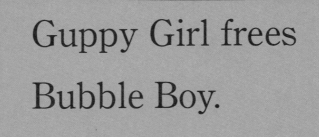

Guppy Girl frees

Bubble Boy.

Bubble Boy blows
a super bubble.
The bubble traps Sid!
Big Bubble City
is safe!

Sid goes to jail.
He thinks no one
wants to be his friend
because he is stinky.

Guppy Girl
and Bubble Boy
have an idea.

"A bubble bath!"
they laugh.
Bubble Boy
and Guppy Girl
save the day!

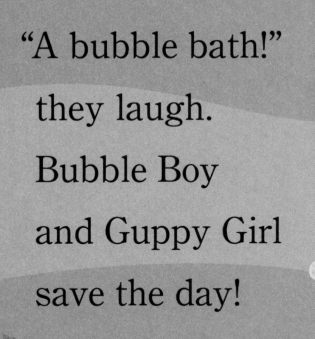